S0-EDI-468

Trick-or-Treatasaurus
Dulce o dinosaurio

Based on the episode "Trick or Treatasaurus" by Bernice Vanderlaan

Adapted by Gabrielle Reyes

Alma's Way © 2021, Think It Through Media, LLC.

All rights reserved. Published by Scholastic Inc., *Publishers since 1920.* SCHOLASTIC and associated logos are trademarks and/or registered trademarks of Scholastic Inc.

The publisher does not have any control over and does not assume any responsibility for author or third-party websites or their content.

No part of this publication may be reproduced, stored in a retrieval system, or transmitted in any form or by any means, electronic, mechanical, photocopying, recording, or otherwise, without written permission of the publisher. For information regarding permission, write to Scholastic Inc., Attention: Permissions Department, 557 Broadway, New York, NY 10012.

This book is a work of fiction. Names, characters, places, and incidents are either the product of the author's imagination or are used fictitiously, and any resemblance to actual persons, living or dead, business establishments, events, or locales is entirely coincidental.

ISBN 978-1-338-89685-5

10 9 8 7 6 5 4 3 2 1   23 24 25 26 27

Printed in the U.S.A.   40

First printing 2023

Book design by Ashley Vargas

Scholastic Inc.

Today is Halloween!

Alma is ready with her costume.

"Make way for the Halloween Train!" she says.

¡Esta noche es Halloween!

Alma ya tiene listo su disfraz.

—¡Abran paso al tren de Halloween! —dice.

Mami sings while she decorates. "Ghosts, bats, and pumpkins, such a spooky sight! Today is Halloween, and I love this spooky night!"

Mami canta mientras pone las decoraciones. —¡Fantasmas, murciélagos y calabazas, qué esperpentos! ¡Esta noche es Halloween y estamos muy contentos!

"Stomp, stomp, stomp," says Junior. "Mami, is it time to go trick-or-treating yet? This Junior-saurus is ready to roar!"

—Pom, pom, pom —dice Junior—. Mami, ¿ya es hora de ir a pedir dulces? ¡Este juniorsaurio está listo para rugir!

"Not yet, my little dino. We can go in two more hours," says Mami. "Let's make some more spooky decorations until then."

—Aún no, mi dinosaurito. Saldremos en un par de horas —dice mami—. Hasta entonces vamos a hacer más adornos escalofriantes.

"Next stop: Decoration Station!" says Alma. "I better take off my train costume. I don't want it to get messy."

—¡Próxima parada, la Estación de Decoración! —dice Alma—. Mejor me quito el disfraz de tren. No quiero que se ensucie.

"What about you, Junior?" asks Mami.
"No, thanks! I'm never taking off my costume!" he says. "Junior-sauruses never get messy."
—¿Y tú, Junior? —pregunta mami.
—¡No, gracias! ¡Nunca me voy a quitar el disfraz! —dice—. Los juniorsaurios nunca se ensucian.

The family goes inside and starts painting.

Alma paints a creepy spider.

Junior paints a scary pumpkin.

Mami paints a spooky ghost.

La familia entra a la casa y comienza a pintar.

Alma pinta una araña horripilante.

Junior pinta una calabaza espeluznante.

Mami pinta un fantasma escalofriante.

Chacho barks suddenly. Mami is startled and messes up her ghost.

"Uh-oh," says Mami.

De repente, Chacho ladra. Mami se asusta y emborrona el fantasma.

—Ay, no —dice mami.

"Aw, your ghost is ruined," says Junior.

—Ay, se arruinó tu fantasma

—dice Junior.

"It is . . ." Mami looks at her painting.
"Or is it?" She smiles.
"Time to work my Halloween magic.
I can turn my ghost into . . .
a ghost-bat!"

—Se… —Mami contempla su pintura—.
¿Estás seguro? —dice sonriendo, y añade—: Es hora de poner
a trabajar mi magia de Halloween. Puedo convertir mi fantasma
en… ¡un murciélago fantasma!

"Your ghost-bat is spooky!" says Junior. "But not as spooky as my pumpkin!"
He shows off his painting.
—¡Tu murciélago fantasma es escalofriante! —dice Junior—. ¡Pero no tanto como mi calabaza!
El niño muestra su pintura.

"Oops! I got paint on my hand!" says Junior. He wipes his hand on his chest. "Oh no!" shouts Junior. "Now I've got paint all over my dinosaur costume! It's ruined!"

—¡Ay! ¡Tengo las manos llenas de pintura! —dice Junior, y se limpia una mano en el pecho—. ¡Oh, no! —grita—. ¡Ahora el disfraz de dinosaurio se me manchó de pintura! ¡Está arruinado!

Junior runs to his bedroom, and Alma follows him.
"I can't wear my costume now," says Junior. "I don't
want to go trick-or-treating anymore."
Junior corre a su habitación, y Alma corre tras él.
—Ahora no puedo usar mi disfraz —dice Junior—. Ya
no quiero ir a pedir dulces.

"I have an idea!" Alma says. "We can find you a different costume." Alma finds a cape.
But Junior doesn't want to be a superhero.

—¡Tengo una idea! —dice Alma—. Podemos hacerte otro disfraz.
Alma encuentra una capa.
Pero Junior no quiere ser un superhéroe.

She finds a construction hat. But Junior doesn't want to be a construction worker.

Alma encuentra un casco. Pero Junior no quiere ser un constructor.

Then Alma finds a pumpkin costume.

"I used to love this costume!" Junior says.

He tries it on, but it's way, way, way too small.

Entonces Alma encuentra un disfraz de calabaza.

—¡Antes me encantaba este disfraz! —dice Junior.

Se lo prueba pero le queda muy, muy, muy chico.

Alma wants to help Junior.
I gotta think about this . . .
Junior really wants to be a
dinosaur, but his costume is
messed up.
Alma quiere ayudar a Junior.
Tengo que pensar...
Alma quiere ayudar a Junior.
Junior quiere mucho ser un dinosaurio,
pero su disfraz se arruinó.

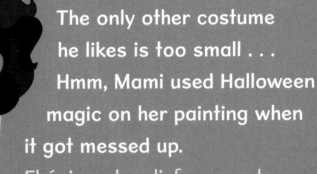

The only other costume
he likes is too small . . .
Hmm, Mami used Halloween
magic on her painting when
it got messed up.
El único otro disfraz que le
gusta le queda muy chico...
Hum, mami usó la magia de Halloween para arreglar
su pintura cuando se arruinó.

"Ooo, magic!" Alma's eyes light up. "I've got a sweet idea! I wonder if we can turn the dinosaur costume into something else . . . I know what to do."

—¡Ay, magia! —A Alma se le ilumina el rostro—. ¡Tengo una idea genial! Me pregunto si podremos convertir el disfraz de dinosaurio en otra cosa… Ya sé qué hacer.

Alma asks for help from her tía Gloria. She's the dino fixer!
"This plan is going to work," Tía Gloria says. She starts her
sewing machine.

Alma le pide ayuda a su tía Gloria. ¡Ella es la arregla
dinosaurios!

—Este plan va a funcionar —dice tía Gloria, y comienza a
coser a máquina.

Later that night, the full moon shines in the dark sky.
Lucas and Rafia arrive for trick-or-treating.
"Wait until you see Junior's new costume!" Alma says.
Al caer la noche, la luna llena brilla en el cielo oscuro.
Lucas y Rafia llegan a pedir dulces.
—¡Deja que vean el nuevo disfraz de Junior! —les dice Alma.

"Stomp, stomp, stomp!" Junior shouts.
"I'm the . . . PUMPKIN-SAURUS! Roar!"
—¡Pom, pom, pom! —grita Junior—.
¡Soy el... CALABAZAURIO! ¡Grrr!

"Pumpkin-saurus? Wow! So cool!" their friends say.

"All aboard the Halloween Train. Next stop: Trick-or-treating!" says Alma.

—¿Calabazaurio? ¡Vaya! ¡Genial! —dicen sus amigos.

—Suban todos al tren de Halloween. ¡Próxima parada, dulce o truco!

—dice Alma.

The friends go all around the neighborhood.
"Trick-ROAR-treat!" says Junior.

Los amigos recorren el vecindario.
—¡Dulce o DINOSAURIO! —dice Junior.

"Junior is so happy with his new costume," Alma says. "I bet he won't take it off until next Halloween!"

—Junior está muy contento con su nuevo disfraz —dice Alma—. ¡Apuesto a que no se lo quita hasta el próximo Halloween!

"Next and final stop on the Halloween Train: Home!" says Alma. "Time to use our magic to make our sweet treats disappear!"

—Próxima y última parada del tren de Halloween: ¡la casa! —dice Alma—. ¡Es hora de usar la magia para hacer desaparecer los dulces!

Alma's Way © 2023
Think It Through Media, LLC.
All rights reserved.

Made in the U.S.A. PO#5104145 04/23